This book contains stereotypes that have been discredited. Students and educators preparing classroom materials should always strive to bring to the educational setting quality literature that is bias free, interesting, and well developed. Please ask a librarian for assistance to determine what titles fit the curriculum and how they might be used to enhance learning.

Daddies

by Lonnie C. Carton

illustrated

by Leslie Jacobs

RANDOM HOUSE · NEW YORK

To the wonderful Daddy of
Paula, Evan and Deborah Ann

Do you know what daddies do when
They go to work each day?
Daddies do so many different
Jobs while they're away!

Daddies work with saws and hammers,
Wrenches, screws and nails;
Daddies work with pens and pencils,
Brushes, paints and pails.

Daddies are the mailmen, teachers,
Grocers, salesmen, cooks.
Daddies work with maps and rulers,
Typewriters and books.

Daddies drive the trucks and cars,
The buses, boats and trains.
Daddies build the roads and bridges,
Houses, stores and planes.

Daddies work in factories and
Daddies make things grow.
Daddies work to figure out
The things we do not know.

Daddies help to make you well and
Keep you safe each day.
Dads make pretty music with
The instruments they play.

Daddies work so long all day, but
When their work is through,
They can hardly wait to hurry home
And be with you!

Then they ride you piggy-back and
Lift you up so high
That you can stretch your arms and
Touch the ceiling if you try.

Daddies give you lots of kisses;
Daddies hug you tight.
But daddies can look angry if
You kick or scream or bite.

Daddies watch you draw and paint and
Make things out of clay.
They listen while you tell them
"Everything" you did all day.

If your blocks keep falling when
You pile them up too high,
Daddies wipe your tears and say,
"Now you're too big to cry."

Some dads smoke a pipe or
A cigar or cigarette.
And they let you blow the match out,
If they don't forget.

Daddies sometimes sit and read
A newspaper or a book;
So if you cannot see their heads,
You know just where to look!

Daddies aren't afraid of noise or
Darkness, bees or snakes,
And they know how to fix up
Almost anything that breaks.

Daddies sit you on their laps,
And read a book or two,
It feels so NICE to have a daddy
Who belongs to you!

Daddies cover up their eyes,
And never try to peek;
But they can always find you when
You're playing hide-and-seek.

Daddies take you up to bed,
And sometimes when they do,
They're the ones who fall asleep in bed,
Instead of you!

When they hear you call them
In the middle of the night,
Daddies bring you water and
Then tuck you in real tight.

Sometimes, in the mornings,
Daddies are such sleepy heads
They won't wake up at all 'til
You start jumping on their beds.

Daddies show you how to
Buckle belts and unknot laces;
Bubbled up with shaving cream,
They make the funniest faces.

Some dads shave with razors that
Make sounds like buzzing bees.
Daddies put on neckties and
They carry lots of keys.

When they take you riding in
A car or train or bus,
Daddies often say, "Sit back!"
"Don't jump around and fuss!"

Daddies lift you up so you can
Reach to mail a letter.
They kiss your bumps and scratches
And make them feel "all better".

Although they do not like to,
Sometimes daddies spank and scold
When you do something naughty,
Or do not do what you're told.

Daddies give you nickels when
You hear the ice cream bell.
Daddies keep your secrets;
And they never, never tell.

Daddies know you're big enough
And brave enough to do
Lots of things that mommies think
Are much too hard for you.

Daddies blow up swimming tubes;
It gets their faces red.
Dads teach you to swim in water
'Way above your head.

Daddies cut and rake the grass,
And Daddies shovel snow.
Daddies sometimes hurry you
Whenever you're too slow.

Dads can answer questions,
'Cause they're smart as they can be.
But, better not ask questions
When they're looking at TV.

Daddies build big snowmen that
Don't crumble up and fall.
Daddies teach you how to catch
And how to throw a ball.

Daddies take their cameras to
The circus, park and zoo.
They take a lot of pictures,
Especially of you!

Daddies sometimes bring home kittens,
Goldfish or a pup.
Pets are fun, but not for Mom,
Who has to "clean things up".

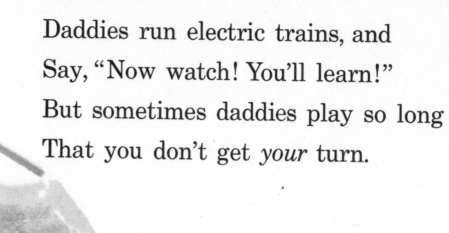

Daddies run electric trains, and
Say, "Now watch! You'll learn!"
But sometimes daddies play so long
That you don't get *your* turn.

Sometimes Daddies let you
Help them find where each piece fits
On puzzles, planes or cars that come
In put-together kits.

You may put on Daddy's shoes and
Make believe you're tall;
But some of Daddy's things you're
Not allowed to touch at all!

Daddies are the bosses!
They mean *NO* when they say "No!"
But they would rather tell you, "Yes!"
Because they love you so!

They love you in the summer,
In the winter, spring and fall;
So when they have to go to work...

THEY MISS *YOU* MOST OF ALL !

Pasture

Garden

Milk house

Back Road — To Pasture and Wood Lot

Farmer Small's Farm
as seen by the eye of a Bird

The Little Farm

THE
LITTLE FARM

LOIS LENSKI

Random House New York

Farmer Small lives
on a farm.
He gets up early
in the morning.

He goes to the barn
to feed the animals.
They are all very
hungry.

He milks the cows.

He strains the milk
into the milk cans.
He sets them in the
milk cooler.

Farmer Small takes the cows to pasture.

Farmer Small leaves
the cans of milk
on the milk stand.
The milk truck takes them
to the dairy.

Farmer Small
feeds the pigs.
They are
very hungry!

So are
the chickens,
the ducks,
and
the turkeys!

At noon,
Farmer Small goes
    to the mailbox
    and gets his mail.

Farmer Small
has a tractor
to help him
with his work.

In the spring,
Farmer Small plows
the field
with his tractor.

He harrows
the field
with his tractor.

In the summer,
Farmer Small
cuts his hay
with his tractor.

He hauls the loads of hay
to the barn.

In the fall,
Farmer Small
  picks apples
  in his orchard.

He hauls them
in the trailer
behind the tractor.

He sells them
at his
roadside stand.

In the winter,
Farmer Small
chops his firewood.

He hauls the wood
on his bobsled
with his team.

Each day,
when evening comes,
Farmer Small gathers
the eggs.

He brings the cows
in from the pasture
and milks them.

Then
he goes into the house
to eat his supper—
and the sun goes down.

*And that's all—
about
Farmer Small!*

0004800105910
EASY LEN
Lenski, Lois,
The little farm /